DANCING WITH SHADES

BOOKS BY D. LIEBER

Minte and Magic

The Exiled Otherkin

The Assassin's Legacy

Intended Fates

Intended Bondmates

Intended Strangers

Intended Enemies

Council of Covens

Dancing with Shades

In Search of a Witch's Soul

Also by D. Lieber

Conjuring Zephyr

Once in a Black Moon

A Very Witchy Yuletide

The Treason of Robyn Hood

The Curse of Moonseed Manor

The Goblin King's Mischief

The Winter Sorcerer and the Summer Witch

Bitten by the North Wind

DANCING WITH SHADES

A COUNCIL OF COVENS NOIR

D. LIEBER

Ink & Magick, LLC
Kenosha, Wisconsin
contact@inkandmagick.com

Paperback ISBN: 978-1-7328323-9-8
Ebook ISBN: 978-1-951239-99-2

Cover by Bryan Donihue, Section 28 Publishing
Edited by Cover to Cover Editing

ONE

S lick with the sweat of nightmares and summer heat, I stared blankly at the morning sun out my opened bedroom window. I shivered, my skin prickling with gooseflesh, while I tried to decide whether to fight the encroaching void that clutched my soul every time I was conscious.

Should I bathe before meeting Jack and Benji today?

Picturing Jack's aquamarine eyes cracked like jagged sea glass as they reflected my pain, I forced my body to sit.

My hand touched the stack of letters on my bed I'd been reading the night before. I stroked the one closest to me and picked it up to read.

March 24, 1918
Dear Caill,

> *We had a little luxury today: hot coffee and*

rum as only a Frenchman can make it. I can't tell you how nice it was to feel a little warmth again.

We had a great excitement yesterday.

We were under fire. The Huns were really bearing down on us. We had given up hope that our reinforcements would come as they were already three days late with no word.

Just when we thought all was lost and the bastards would reach our trench, a great violet cloud engulfed the advancing Germans.

I barely had time to put my gas mask on when the sergeant choked out his order to do so.

After much shouting and coughing, silence took the field. I couldn't hear anything for a long time over my own breathing, and of course I couldn't see through the gas.

All of a sudden, a platoon of doughboys dropped into our trench! They had moved so quietly, my heart nearly leapt from my chest.

It was some of the Hell Fire Boys from the 30th Engineer Regiment, the all-witch unit who use their knowledge of magic and potions to fight the good fight.

You should have seen the cheeky grin the fella who dropped in beside me wore. He let out a laugh and clapped me on the shoulder. "Sorry we're late" was what he said.

And I have to admit, the lot of us were relieved they came before it was too late.

It seems we will be moving on with the Hell Fire Boys for a while. This fella is called Victor, and he seems the friendly sort. I think we will get along great.

I know you're back home missing me, but don't worry. These bastards won't get the best of me.

Keep your arms warm for me

You're in my heart always,
Love Cy

I closed my eyes against the telltale burn of oncoming tears. *But I'm not in your heart, am I, Cy? You left me behind, and I will never see you again.*

Shaking my head, I tried to swallow the memories of my dead soulmate. I took a deep breath and thought about how I would see him again if all went well with Benji.

After bathing and dressing in light clothes, I went down to breakfast.

Dad looked twice when he glanced up at me over his newspaper. Aunt Vi pretended not to notice though I saw the relief in the smoothness of her brow.

"Good morning, my girl. You have plans today?" Dad asked as I forced myself to nibble on a piece of toast.

I nodded. "I'm meeting Jack this morning."

"So Jackie Boy is in town, is he?"

"Yeah, he's on break, so he wanted to get together."

Dad bobbed his head. "I was going to ask your help with a case I'm working, but if you're going with Jackie Boy..." he trailed off.

I stared into my orange juice, stifling my tears. *I know, Dad. I want to get better. I do. I don't want my pain to hurt you all anymore.*

"Maybe I will come by the office later," I hedged, not knowing how my meeting with Benji would go.

He gave me a soft smile, his eyes crinkling at the corners, and it warmed my heart.

"What's your case about?" Aunt Vi asked.

We both looked at her sharply, knowing how she felt about talking cases at the table.

Dad cleared his throat. "Oh, uh. A lady came in a few days ago, wanting us to find out what her son is up to. Seems he's been acting suspicious lately: coming and going at all hours, lying, flushed with dough. She's under the impression he's gotten himself into some trouble, possibly gambling."

"But that should be easy enough. Just follow him," I suggested.

Aunt Vi's eyes sparkled over her cup of joe at my interest.

Dad scratched his unshaven chin. "That's the trouble, see. I know where he's going to be, but I wouldn't be able to blend in there. Now, my pretty twenty-year-old daughter? No one would suspect her."

"All right, I get the picture. I'll see what I can do about helping you out."

"I knew I could count on my girl."

"Yeah, yeah. Don't get ahead of yourself. No guarantees."

"I'm sure you'll be all fired up to work when you

hear all the things Jackie Boy has been up to at college."

That certainly would have been true of the old me. "Speaking of whom, I better blouse, or I'll be late."

Leaving most of my breakfast uneaten, I ankled to the door.

They called their I-love-yous after me, and I responded in kind.

TWO

The hot August sun bore down on me as I walked the dusty city streets. Even the school children had abandoned their summertime games in favor of the cool shade of the concrete alleyways.

The exhausting oppression of the weather didn't really have an effect on me. I was already drained of motivation and energy. In fact, I found it refreshing to be able to wear my exhaustion, everyone blaming the heat.

I found Jack, tall and lean, at the docks, just where he'd said he would be. His eyes sparkled in the sunshine like the glittering water behind him. He hadn't been home in a few weeks, and the weight in my chest lightened when I saw his smile.

Jack's attention was directed at a woman in a blue kneeduster, his smile meant for her.

His throaty chuckle made me stop short. "Yeah? I may have to come by," he said, pausing to smile at her again. "Will you be there, too?"

The woman giggled. "Maybe. Would you like that?" she flirted.

My stomach rolled. Feeling like an imposition, I took a step back.

Just when I turned to go, Jack's gaze flicked in my direction. His face broke into a brilliant grin. "Anna!" he called gleefully, rushing over and wrapping me in a crushing hug.

His joy made my heart weightless, and I was at peace if only for a moment.

"Hey, Jack," I murmured. "It's been a while."

The smile slid from his face when I didn't get my tone just right. I flinched as his eyes took me in.

"Thanks for coming out to see me, Anna," he said gently as if I'd break.

"Lay off, Jack. You're my best friend. Of course, I want to see you."

He frowned. "I'm sorry I haven't been home much lately. It's just—"

I tried for a smile. "Don't worry about it, Jack. You've got school and everything. Why don't you tell me what you've been up to? Starting with your friend over there."

Jack glanced over his shoulder at the woman in the blue skirt as if he'd forgotten she was there. She didn't hide her pouting lips, but she managed to make the glare she shot at me almost imperceptible.

"Ah, this is Molly. We just met while I was waiting for you. I've got other plans now, Molly, but maybe I'll come to that blow you mentioned before."

Molly bit her lip. "Well aren't you just full of

applesauce," she huffed. She didn't even glance in our direction as she strode away.

I glanced at Jack, eyebrows raised. "Well...aren't you going after her?"

He shrugged. "No, I made plans with you. You still want to go fishing, don't you?"

I smiled easily. "Yeah, did you bring everything?"

Jack directed me to the fishing tackle. After getting our rods ready, we sat at the edge of the dock. We were quiet for a long time, watching the lines in the easy waves and listening to the bustle of the pier. People crowded the shoreline, enjoying the breeze off the lake, the only respite from the heat. The crew of a cargo ship loaded and unloaded their freight, shouting orders at each other.

"How's school?" I asked just wanting to hear his voice.

"It's going well. My writing professors are helpful, and I just joined the university's newspaper."

"Yeah, you said that in your last letter."

"I guess I did," he agreed, then paused. "Have you started working with your dad again?"

"I help by answering the telephone and meeting with clients, but I haven't taken on any more cases yet."

He frowned at this admission.

"Actually, Dad asked for my help on a case he is working now. I'll probably help him later," I soothed. "You said you were going to see your sister today, right?"

He nodded, not convinced. After another long

pause, he turned to me, his eyes sad and vulnerable and his shoulders slumped. "Anna," he said huskily, then cleared his throat. "How are you really?"

I didn't move, didn't speak. I just stared at my line, breathing slowly.

"I'm fine," I murmured, not even convincing myself.

"You're lying," Jack accused.

I didn't have to agree; we both knew he was right.

Jack wrapped his arm around my shoulders and rested his head on mine. "I'm here," he whispered.

My eyes swam.

"I'm here, Anna. I will always be here. Whenever and however you need me," he promised.

Tears spilling over, I swallowed my sob. "Jack..." I whimpered.

He squeezed me tighter.

"Jack, he died hating me."

"No," Jack argued immediately. "That's not true, Anna. He loved you. You know he did. Why would you even think something like that?"

I can't tell Jack that Cy hated me because of him. We were all friends for so long; it would break Jack's heart. "We fought before he died," I admitted. "He—"

I took a steadying breath.

"He even broke it off with me before he left that night."

Jack was silent as he put some of the pieces together of what had happened. "I'm sorry, Anna. I didn't know. But even if that's true, I can't believe he could ever hate you. I told you he would come back from the war different. Perhaps he just needed time to readjust."

His words sounded good, solid and logical. But he didn't know what I knew; he hadn't heard what the medium had said. *And he never will.*

THREE

Entering Pliski's Pharmacy, I tried to bury my conversation with Jack. *Just a little longer. I'll be able to bear it all after today.*

I asked the soda jerk behind the counter for a Pepsi-Cola, wanting to settle my nervous stomach. Sitting on the high stool, I hadn't taken two sips before someone slid onto the seat beside me.

"This heat could kill a man," Benji complained, fanning himself with his boater.

I glanced at him but didn't respond.

"How's my favorite human?" he asked, tilting his head with a smirk.

I rolled my eyes. "Your favorite?"

"Of course, Doll. Who else?"

"You must not know many humans."

He smiled. "That's entirely beside the point."

After looking around the pharmacy, Benji beckoned to the jerk and asked for a "dark star."

The jerk nodded, then motioned us toward the

swinging door over his shoulder.

"Let's go," Benji suggested, gently grabbing my elbow and leading me through to the small, deserted storage room.

After releasing my arm, Benji went to the back wall and easily slid the shelves to one side as if they were on wheels. Behind the stocked shelves was a wooden door with chipped paint that could have once been called green.

The door led to a small courtyard surrounded by the other buildings that shared the block. Tall, brick walls closed the courtyard in, not even windows facing it.

I followed Benji to an ordinary manhole cover at the center of the enclosed space.

"You ready?" he asked.

I shrugged in indifference despite my heart pounding. Benji smiled and gave me a wink as if he could hear it. With his palms held out before him, he pronounced the words of magic, and the heavy cover lifted and slid to one side.

Sweeping his hand in the direction of the cold, dark hole, he said, "Ladies first."

I straightened my spine and approached the entrance to Starlight Avenue with feigned confidence. Climbing down the ladder to the magical underground, the cold iron chilled my fingers as my shoes rang on the metal in the dark.

As soon as my feet met stone, an icy dread made me shiver like a ghost breath on the back of my neck. I fought the dizziness that crept over me, knowing it was only the enchantments on the secret place.

Once Benji was standing beside me, he replaced the hole's cover with a magic-laced word. The only source of light taken, I held my breath as more of Benji's magical whispers echoed off the earthen walls. At his command, a violet will-o'-the-wisp glowed into existence before our eyes.

The creeping terror subsided in the light of our guide, and I sighed.

"Don't worry, Honey. I'll keep you safe from the things that lurk in the shadows," Benji teased.

"Gee, thanks," I muttered, not quite sure how serious he was as we followed our guide through the dark tunnels.

As we turned a corner, I blinked against the brightness of the electric lights lining a tunnel full of doors.

"Looks like they're building up the place after all," Benji commented, marking the atmospheric improvements.

Tailing the glowing orb of violet light, we meandered through the tunnels, some lit but most not, until it melted into a cream-colored door.

Benji pressed his hand to the wood, and it unlocked with a faint click. At the bottom of a flight of stairs, the door locked behind us. Benji motioned me to wait as he went on ahead.

Out of sight, Benji called to someone above, and I held my breath to listen.

"Benjamin Wilkenson. I didn't think I'd ever see your broomstick on my porch again," a woman greeted, the smile evident in her voice.

"Lillian, you grow as beautiful as a wild rose," Benji complimented,

"Oh ho! What's with the flattery, Benji? You must have come for a favor."

"You are as sharp as ever, Lillian. I need you to perform Living Memory."

Lillian paused, then lowered her voice. "Did something happen? What could you have forgotten that's so important?"

"It's not for me, Lillian, but a friend, a human in fact."

Lillian's answering silence had me straining my ears. "Benji..." she hesitated. "Magic is illegal in front of humans per the 18th Amendment. You know that."

"I do, but I also know it's an unfair law aimed specifically at persecuting us again. Half your business was to cater to humans. Don't tell me you aren't hurting. And Lillian, this is important."

"I don't know, Benji...Who is this human?"

"Her name is Anna Caill. I met her at Henry Hartley's birthday party."

"Henry Hartley? Are you still hanging around him? His father is a copper."

"And he and his family have always been kind to us, copper or not," Benji said as if reminding her.

"So this friend is a friend of Henry's?"

"They seem to have known each other for a long while. Their fathers are friends."

Silence answered this statement. "This friend also the kid of a copper then?"

"No, a dick."

"Are you serious, Benji?" Lillian raised her voice.

"Yeah, and she's training with him to be one herself."

"What is wrong with you? Why would you bring someone like that to Starlight Avenue, let alone into my home?"

Benji's voice became hard and serious. "You think I didn't take precautions? I even hit her with a truth spell. She's a good person, Lillian, and she's in pain. You can see it in her eyes. She's broken and beat, and you could help her. Her soulmate broke the bond between their souls."

Lillian's answer was hushed. "Benji, I'm sorry your friend is hurting, I truly am. No one should have to endure that kind of pain. But even if this person was a witch and my personal friend, I wouldn't administer Living Memory under those circumstances. It's addictive. If she uses it in that state of grief, she may never come out."

"She will. I know she will. She's broken, but she has the will to live, if not fully at least functionally."

"Benji..."

"Alice told me to bring her here."

Lillian paused for a long while. "Alice?"

Benji must have nodded because after another pause, Lillian sighed. "I don't think this is a good idea, but if Alice told you to bring her...I trust Alice's judgement. Your friend is welcome here. Bring her whenever you want."

"She's here now," Benji admitted. "Anna," he called down to me. "You can come up now."

FOUR

I climbed the stairs, cringing at having listened to their entire conversation, and entered into a cozy sitting room. Lillian was a tall witch with long, wild hair and a flowing gown. Her presence was solid and demanding as she laughed in the face of modern fashion.

Her expression was smooth and formal, but not cold, as Benji introduced us.

"You're here for a Living Memory spell?" she asked.

I nodded.

"Do you know what that spell entails?"

"Alice told me I could relive memories of my soulmate."

"Yes, but there are side effects. For every pleasant memory you relive, you will also relive an equally unpleasant memory when you next sleep."

"When I relive these memories, will it feel real?" I asked.

She frowned. "It will feel as though it is happening, yes."

I can see Cy again? I can hear his voice? I can feel his touch? Worth it. Any pain would be worth that. "I understand the side effects. I still want the spell," I told Lillian.

"Did Alice tell you how addictive this spell can be?"

"She did."

Lillian sighed in resignation. "Very well. I have not yet disassembled my workroom. Benji, wait here. Anna, you can follow me."

I did as Lillian bid me and followed her up the stairs to a third-floor observatory. The round room had a peaked roof and large windows. Work benches were covered in jars and bowls filled with dark liquids and mysterious powders. An altar stood in the center of the room, its candles burning even in the heat of summer. I coughed as I inhaled the incense smoke floating like wispy clouds.

"I suppose I should be more careful with how much incense I use in the future," Lillian commented by way of conversation. "What with it being illegal now."

"It seems the magical community is still in full operation even with the prohibition. It may be more difficult to get ahold of, but I'm sure you'll still be able to get it," I reassured her.

She paused and eyed me. Then she gave me a small smile and a nod.

She motioned for me to rest on a long divan. "Lie here, and please remove your shoes."

I stretched out, resting my head on the plush cushion she'd provided. My heart hammered in my ears, and I strained to hear her over it.

"This spell can work one of two ways. You can either concentrate on a memory you'd like to relive, or you can allow your mind to choose based on an idea or desire. I suggest, as this is your first time, you choose a simple memory that you already remember quite well."

"All right," I acknowledged, trying to think of a simple, happy memory and landing on one of a summer's day some ten years prior.

Lillian stood at my head and breathed deep the magic-enhancing incense smoke. After a few moments, she looked down and met my eyes.

"Are you certain?" she asked in a voice that almost had me questioning my decision.

I need to see him. This is the only way. "I'm certain," I declared.

"Very well. Close your eyes and think of that memory. Who was there? What were you doing? How did it start? Picture that in your mind. Feel it."

We were so excited that day. It was early summer, not as hot as today. Some of the older kids had told Cy we could play baseball with them. The only condition was that I bring the bat Dad had given me. Its solid weight rested on my shoulder as Cy, Jack, and I walked to the empty lot to meet the older kids.

～

"How many fellas did you say there were, Cy?" Jack asked as we neared the lot.

Cy shrugged. "I don't remember. Six maybe? I was just walking by after my dance lesson and saw them playing."

"But why would they invite us?" Jack asked.

"Who cares, Jack? We can finally play with more people. It'll be way more fun than just the three of us," Cy argued.

Jack and I agreed.

As we reached our destination, we stopped to observe, our mouths agape. The older kids, some two and three years our seniors, were already getting ready for the game. They had only three mitts between them, a dusty ball, and a two by two piece of wood, which they used as a bat. Their lack of equipment didn't hinder their skills.

"Hey, fellas," Cy called, and they turned in our direction.

Cy straightened to his full height, thrusting his chest out. "I told ya we'd come," he boasted.

"Yeah? Did you bring the bat?" a tall boy with freckles challenged.

"I did," I answered, stepping up beside Cy with my prized possession.

The group of boys' eyes widened, and they stared in silence. Then they burst into laughter.

"Is that a girl?" the freckled kid asked between snickers.

"No way," another answered. "He's wearing trousers and suspenders."

I looked down at my clothes, not seeing anything wrong. They were the same as Dad's.

"Yeah, she is," a third argued. "Look at her long hair."

I frowned, touching my unbound waves.

"What's so funny?" Cy demanded.

"You didn't tell us your friend with the bat was a girl," the first kid sneered. "Girls can't play baseball."

"So what if Caill is a girl. She's great at baseball. She's probably better than all of you," Cy defended.

The boys roared with laughter. A strange and unfamiliar feeling came over me. I dropped my gaze.

Jack's warm hand squeezed my shoulder. "Don't listen to them, Anna. You have nothing to prove to them. We know you're a great baseball player. We can just take your bat and play at home like always. Nothing they say will take your talent away."

I sniffed hard and straightened my back. "You're right, Jack. I am good at baseball, and I'm going to prove it."

Cy grinned in triumph, and Jack smiled in encouragement.

"You fellas aren't scared of losing to a girl, are you?" Cy taunted.

Resurfacing from the partial memory, Cy's unwavering confidence in me remained. I felt as if I'd just seen him, as if he'd only left the room moments before. The heavy knot in my chest loosened, and I took a deep, unhindered breath for the first time in months.

It wasn't like I'd forgotten Cy was dead; my mind knew it quite clearly. Rather, it was more my heart, my soul, my body had just seen him, just heard his laughter. He wasn't gone. He was very much within me, and I could see him anytime I wanted. Though somewhere I knew, it wasn't the same as before.

FIVE

Paying Lillian for her services was kale well-spent. Neither Lillian nor Benji seemed surprised by the change in me, but Benji at least looked pleased.

I wouldn't say I was happy after my experience, it was more like the pain was dulled. My mind no longer trudged through the brambled paths of mental agony. I could think again. Cold and silent, still empty, but I could think.

Yes, this is workable. I can pretend like this. I can be functional for them like this.

As Benji and I trailed a newly created will-o'-the-wisp back through Starlight Avenue, I found my senses sharper than before. The light from the guide penetrated farther into the tunnel's darkness. The edges of the many doors leading to magical shops and services were sharp and clear. My ears twitched at the scuffle of our shoes as they echoed down unseen paths. The fog of grief had dissipated though it still hung about in the hollows of my mind, waiting for the sun of Living Memory to set.

The guide melted into a pink door, which I followed Benji through. I raised an eyebrow at him when I found us in a water closet.

He smiled and shrugged, exiting the other door. Behind us, the entrance to Starlight Avenue blended into the striped floral wallpaper with three-dimensional roses, the door handle cleverly concealed as a rose.

Tall shelves of records lined the walls from floor to ceiling. The horn of a phonograph wailed jazz brass and drums in the corner. A flapper in a knee-length skirt with her stockings rolled down leaned on the clerk's counter, a dincher wafting between her fingers.

Benji tipped his hat to the woman, who smiled lazily as we walked on through her shop.

I hadn't realized how cool the tunnels of Starlight Avenue had been until we stepped out into the midday sunshine.

"Where are you off to?" Benji asked, breaking the silence of our awkward goodbyes.

"To help my dad on a case," I told him, up for working for the first time since losing Cy.

He nodded. "I'm glad to hear it. And listen, don't be a stranger. You can always come to me."

"Thanks, Benji, but how will I find you?"

"Oh, I'll be around when you need me," he smirked.

"How did I ever deserve a friend like you?" I asked in a moment of honest gratitude. "If you or anyone else in the magical community ever needs a PI, you can count on me."

The witch gave me a charming smile and ran his fingertip along the brim of his boater. "That's how. Even drowning in your own personal Hell, you think of others. You've got a good heart, Anna. I just hope I can see it heal someday."

I tried for a smile, which likely looked a little sad, knowing deep down my heart would never fully heal.

"There's my favorite human. Keep your chin up, Kid. We'll make it through."

I will survive to see another day at least.

Benji and I parted ways outside the record shop. Though no promises were made, I knew we'd see each other again even if I didn't know exactly when.

I dodged motorcars in the street and hopped a streetcar heading farther into downtown. I took a seat near the back and rested my temple against the window jamb. The breeze from the car's movement wasn't much, but it was pleasant nonetheless.

The building our office was in had that dirty gray look like an old dime dropped in a storm drain: still useful and nothing really wrong with it, but something tells you to leave it be. The stairs creaked as I climbed to the second floor, bits of debris and grime collected in the corners where the landlady hadn't bothered.

I entered the frosted door labelled Caill Detective Agency, and Dad looked up from his desk, his pipe clenched between his teeth. His eyes lit up, and he grinned behind a puff of smoke.

"You're here, my girl."

"I am," I agreed, sitting in the chair across his desk and leaning my chin on my laced fingers. "How can I help?"

"You ever been to a juke joint called John Boy's?"

I nodded. "A few times. Booze, music, and dancing mostly. Haven't been there since Prohibition started. Is that where our fella is going to be?"

Dad nodded and pushed a photograph across the desk to me. "His name is Peter, but he goes by Pip."

I looked at the clean-cut youth in his Sunday best. He stood on the last stoop of an average apartment building. A little girl with ribbons and lace held his hand from the step above.

"His sister?" I asked.

Dad nodded.

I stared at the photograph, memorizing his face. His eyes, so full of innocence, struck me, and I whispered, "What have you gotten yourself into, Pip?"

SIX

Before heading to John Boy's that evening, I went home to doll up. I put on my best glad rags: a creamy yellow dress with a flame orange sash. The colors flattered my complexion and chestnut hair and would blend in more with the gaiety of the crowd than something more subdued.

I arrived at the joint well after dark just when the place hit full capacity. The flappers, the floorflushers, the cake eaters, the sips, the sharpshooters, all crowded the dance floor, hopping to the wild tunes the band blasted from the stage.

"Get hot! Get hot!" one fella yelled to a wiggling woman.

The atmosphere washed over me, and I paused for a moment, overwhelmed. I hadn't been to a place like that since the night Cy died, and I knew I wouldn't have been able to handle it were it not for Living Memory. The din settled into my ears, and I adjusted after a deep breath.

After slipping through the crowd to the bar, I asked for a bee's knees. I sipped my drink at the corner of the bar near the stairs, scanning the room for Pip.

It wasn't long before some beasel hound approached me asking for my name. I opened my mouth to tell him I wasn't interested when my gaze caught sight of my mark over his left shoulder.

Pip looked much older than his photograph, not in age but in experience. His hair was oiled and his suit crisp. He had none of that Sunday school innocence while he ordered a whiskey on the rocks.

"I said, what's your name, Doll?" asked the man who'd approached me.

Pip looked over at the fella's tone.

I clicked my tongue but smiled and answered. "Minnie. How about you?"

Pip lost interest when there wasn't a confrontation.

The fella chatting at me responded, but I was too busy watching Pip to hear him. Lucky for me, whatever-his-name-was seemed to be a high cloud who could talk about himself for hours without help. I nodded at him while he went on, following Pip with my eyes as he sat alone at a nearby table, his gaze fixed on the drink he clutched.

Near me, a fella with a green hat band came down the stairs. I pursed my lips, recognizing him without being able to place him. He saw Pip and approached him.

Pip looked up and jumped to his feet. The fella stepped in close.

Pip's eyes were wide and nervous, darting around as he said something with a bowed head. The fella reached out and grabbed a fistful of Pip's jacket, curling his lips as he made his point.

Pip nodded quickly, showing he understood the man's threat. The fella shoved Pip back into his chair and pointed a finger at him.

Straightening his suit, the fella headed back toward me. I turned my attention to my chatty cover.

"So I told him: hey, Pal, it's not my fault the Jane prefers me," he argued as I feigned interest.

Pip's friend slipped by and started up the stairs. I peeked at his retreating form over the rim of my glass. My heart jumped, and I nearly choked when I saw who stood at the top of the stairs.

Slim Frank looked down at the fella as he approached. He wore his signature pin-striped suit and held a martini and a ciggy in one hand. Frank Luciano, also known as Slim Frank, ran the Druzina, a magical organization that specialized in the rare and illegal.

That would make Pip's friend Frank's second in command, Bobby the Boomslang. I knew he looked familiar. I sighed and shook my head, directing my attention back to my target. *Oh, Pip. You're in over your head.*

Pip stood from his seat, downed his whiskey, and strode toward the exit.

I put my glass on the bar and turned to my shield. "If you'll excuse me. I need to take the air." I didn't wait to hear his response but followed Pip through the crowd.

Even on the sticky summer night, the fresh air felt cooler than in the crowded bar. I caught sight of Pip just as he was turning a corner to a back alley. Picking up my pace, I called out to him when he was about halfway to the other side.

He turned around at his name and eyed me. "Do I know you?"

I caught up to him and shook my head. "No, you don't, but I'm here to help."

He turned to leave. "I don't need your help."

I grabbed his arm. "Your mother is worried about you, Pip. These are dangerous men you're involved with. We don't want you to get hurt."

He tensed under my hand but didn't turn. I walked around to face him. He hung his head, his eyes shadowed in the dim lamplight.

"There's nothing you can do," he murmured.

"Listen," I hushed. "I'm a PI. I can help you get out."

He met my gaze, and I saw fear in his shaking eyes.

"You think I haven't tried to get out? I'm in way too deep. They'll never let me go."

I stroked his arm, trying to soothe him. "I have contacts with the police. If you tell them what you know, they can protect you and your family."

Doubt crept into his expression, and he bit his lip. "Who do you think I'm doing this for? Mom, Willow, someone has to take care of them since Dad left." Shaking his head, he said, "No, no coppers. They'll only make things worse. The Druzina are too good. They've greased too many palms. It'll never stick, and then we'll all be in trouble." He shook off my hand.

"We can help you," I reasserted. "Just think about it. All right? Meet me at the docks at two a.m."

"Leave me alone," he urged, striding away from me.

"I'll be waiting for you," I called after him.

SEVEN

Retreating back the way I'd come, I thought about what I should do next. *I need to catch Dad up on what's going on. But will Pip meet me? The fear in his eyes was real, but so was his desire to protect his family.* I sighed. *I guess I'll just have to wait and see.*

I took the last nightcar to the docks, hoping for the best. The breeze off the lake was almost cold when I stepped off the nearly empty streetcar. The docks were a ghostly echo of the flurry they had been earlier that day.

The light from the streetlamps on the pier didn't even reach the low spring tide of the lake below. And the lighthouse farther out in the harbor struggled to fulfill its duty as a summer fog rolled in.

My heels on the pier were too loud in the night as I approached a payphone. I asked the operator to connect me to Chestnut 3-6023, my hushed voice resounding in my ears.

Aunt Vi answered, hoarse from being pulled from bed.

"Hello?"

"Aunt Vi? It's Anna. Listen, is Dad home?"

She paused, likely looking to see if his hat and shoes were there.

"It doesn't appear so. Where are you, Anna? It's late. You should be home."

"I'm helping Dad on that case he told us about this morning. Can you track him down for me? Let him know I'm supposed to meet Pip at the docks at two. It seems he got in too deep with the Druzina."

She gasped. "I'll call around right now. Maybe he's still at the office."

"I hope so. Thanks, Aunt Vi."

I hung the earpiece back in its cradle.

I knew I still had time before I'd asked Pip to meet me. I stood under a streetlamp, so he could easily find me. The sound of the waves and the fog creeping toward the shore lulled me into a state of meditation.

"What's your business here, Miss?" a night-watchman demanded, pulling me from my thoughts.

I blinked, not sure how much time had passed. Assuming my best innocent face, I pleaded with the man. "Oh, I'm sorry, Sir. I ain't here to bother nothin'. I just love looking at the lake at night. It's so beautiful. Can't I just stay a little longer? I won't hurt nothin'. I promise."

The watchman looked me up and down and smiled. "All right, Sweetheart. You can stay, but be careful, will ya? Call out if you have any trouble."

I smiled prettily at him. "Of course, Sir. Thank you."

He tipped his hat to me and continued his patrol.

I sighed and looked to the street, hoping Pip would soon make an appearance. I wasn't disappointed. The youth came out of the shadows, looking over his shoulder every few seconds. He found me with ease and skittered toward me.

"I'm glad you came," I told him once he'd reached me.

"I've still got a bad feeling about this," he admitted.

"Don't worry. We'll protect you. The coppers have been trying to put an end to the Druzina for a while."

He nodded. "The Druzina have only grown more powerful since Prohibition, and they've got big plans in the works."

"Are they expanding their business?"

"You could say that. They're building an entire exchange for illegal goods. Artisans and dealers, all in one place."

"I can guess who gets a cut off the top."

He nodded. "They call it—" Pip's hurried whispers cut off abruptly, and his eyes widened.

"What is it? Are you all right?" I asked, alarmed by his expression.

He began to cough, a deep, wet sound between heaving breaths. He dropped to all fours, hacking and fighting for air.

I knelt beside him, uncertain of what I could do. Looking around frantically, I saw a male form wearing a green hat band stroll away into the night.

I shifted to chase after him, but Pip rose to his knees, grabbing my wrists.

"Don't," he managed to murmur, blood trickling from his nose.

His frightened eyes were wide and full of red tears. His next cough spewed blood on the front of my dress.

"Tell Mom and Willow...I love them..." He looked down at the blood soaking his nice suit. "And...don't...don't let them see me like this."

I screamed for help as he was overcome by the spell again.

The nightwatchman arrived just as Pip let out his last gurgling breath. His blue eyes were no longer innocent or scared just still and empty.

EIGHT

Dad arrived only minutes before the coppers. He rushed to where I stood with the night-watchman, my arms wrapped around myself. Placing his jacket on my shoulders, he covered my crimson-speckled yellow dress, then pulled me into his arms.

My deep breath came out a shudder. "I shouldn't have pushed him to meet me..." I said, my voice thin and void of emotion.

He hushed me, gently stroking my hair. "Don't you take that onto yourself, my girl. The boy wouldn't have met you if he hadn't wanted to."

"I told him we could protect him."

"If they used magic, there's nothing you could have done to save him."

Dad's friend, Detective Albert Hartley, approached us.

"Seems the boy was in deep with the Druzina," Dad said.

Ace nodded. "We've known about him for a little while, but I'm sorry he ended up like this."

"Fellas like that give witches a bad name."

"The press is going to be all over this," Ace agreed.

"Will you be able to catch the men who did this?" I asked Ace.

The detective met my eyes steadily. "Your dad tells me you want to be a PI."

I nodded.

"Then here's a hard lesson for you, Kid. Things don't always go to plan, and sometimes the guilty get away with it. The fellas we're dealing with are well-protected both magically and legally. They have friends in high places. We can build our case, but we may never catch them."

The truth settled into my stomach and hardened.

"Don't let it stop you from trying," Ace encouraged, patting me on the shoulder.

Dad and I promised to come to the station the following day to give full statements, and then Dad drove us home. We didn't speak except to say goodnight once inside.

By the time I'd washed and changed for bed, I was so exhausted I had forgotten what Lillian had told me about Living Memory's side effects.

I buried my face in my coat against the winter wind as I entered Centre Station with Cy and Jack. My shallow breaths kept the cold air from my lungs and my tears at bay.

Just hold out a little longer. He hates it when you cry.

I would have lost Cy in a sea of olive drab had I not been holding his hand. It seemed all the men were off to war. *Well, all except Jack, thank goodness.*

Every step we took closer to the platform seemed a step closer to Cy's death. I knew my whole life would change the moment he got on that train. I wrestled with my anxiety and thoughts of his impending doom as he pulled me along. Jack followed behind.

"Look at those long faces!" Cy teased, stopping on the platform where his train waited.

Jack stepped up and held out his hand, which Cy shook. "You be careful over there. I wish I was going with you. But who knows? If the war goes long enough, maybe I'll be twenty-one before it's over."

"Sure, but keep working on that parental consent. There's no way we won't give those Huns a swift defeat."

Cy turned to me. "Come on, Caill. Give me a smile."

I sighed and tried my best.

"That's my girl. Come here."

He opened his arms to me, and I squeezed him tight.

"You'll write me?" I asked, looking up pleadingly.

"Of course I will." He smiled.

When he pressed his lips to mine, I thought my heart would burst. I poured all my love into him, willing him to return home safely.

"Whoa," he gasped. "You trying to warm me up for the entire time I'm gone?" He grinned. "You make me want to stay. Save me one like that for when I get home."

I bit my lip and nodded, already feeling empty without his embrace.

Shouldering his rucksack, he gave us a cocky smile and winked. "I'll be home soon," he promised.

Then he boarded the train without looking back. The moment he was out of sight, my knees wobbled and gave out. Jack caught me before I hit the ground.

"Jack," I sobbed, not able to keep my tears at bay any longer.

"I know," he hushed, wrapping me in his arms.

My heart screamed out its pain, and it was all I could do just to breathe.

I awoke, my soul wailing for my lost love. All the relief Living Memory had given me the day before was gone, and my agony felt worse than it had before I'd experienced the spell.

Shaking with heart-wrenching sorrow, one clear thought came to mind.

I need to use Living Memory again.

AFTERWORD

Thank you for reading! I do so hope you enjoyed it. If you have a moment, I would very much appreciate a review on the store where you bought it. Tell other readers what you thought, and help them make a decision on this book.

If you'd like to stay updated on news about my books and events, you can subscribe to my newsletter on my website: www.dlieber.com

On my site, you will also find my blog, where I post all my fun little tidbits.

Thanks again! I hope you will travel through my worlds with me again in the future.

D. Lieber

IN SEARCH OF A WITCH'S SOUL

A COUNCIL OF COVENS NOIR

D. LIEBER

IN SEARCH OF A WITCH'S SOUL
BY D. LIEBER

A dark spell that promises sweet memories. Will she give up her future just to endure her present?

At the turn of 1920, magical prohibition went into effect. A year later, human private detective-in-training Anna Caill needs a spell. She knows what it will cost, and she's ready to take the risks, despite the warnings.

She can't survive another day swallowed by the despair she's felt since losing her soul mate, and this spell is the only chance she has of living any sort of functional life for the people who still care for her. The steep consequences are tomorrow's problem.

As Anna gets her first hit of the dark spell that even witches hesitate to use, she finds the cold peace she needs to take on cases in this urban fantasy noir.

"Love is always magical; and nothing blows hot and cold like a witch's soul. This is a magical book with a whole lot of soul." — Simon R. Green, author of the *Nightside* series

D. Lieber has a wanderlust that would make a butterfly envious. When she isn't planning her next physical adventure, she's recklessly jumping from one fictional world to another. Her love of reading led her to earn a Bachelor's in English from Wright State University.

Beyond her skeptic and slightly pessimistic mind, Lieber wants to believe. She has been many places—from Canada to England, France to Italy, Germany to Russia—believing that a better world comes from putting a face on "other." She is a romantic idealist at heart, always fighting to keep her feet on the ground and her head in the clouds.

Lieber lives in Wisconsin with her husband (John) and cats (Yin and Nox).

Links:

Website: www.dlieber.com

Goodreads: www.goodreads.com/dlieberwriting

BookBub: https://www.bookbub.com/profile/d-lieber

www.ingramcontent.com/pod-product-compliance
Lightning Source LLC
Chambersburg PA
CBHW050159110726
47898CB00008B/2866